THE PROPHET MU[illegible]D

(upon hi[illegible]ngs)

b[illegible]

Retold by Ahmed Abo Khegar

Illustrated by Mohsen Abou al-Azm

with calligraphy by Abdelghani Azzi

genç kaknüs

REAL READS

kaknüs publications: 681
young kaknus series: 06

isbn: 978-975-256-488-6
publishers certificate no: 11216

first edition in türkiye: 2017
printed in ankara, türkiye by ertem inc.
graphic design: lucy guenot

kaknüs publications
kızkulesi yayıncılık eğitim san. tic. ltd. şti.
chief office: mimar sinan mah., selami ali efendi cad., no: 5, üsküdar, istanbul
phone: (+90 216) 341 08 65 - 492 59 74/75 fax: 334 61 48
kitap@kaknus.com.tr
distribution: çatalçeşme sk., defne han, no: 27/3, cağaloğlu, istanbul
phone: (+90 212) 520 49 27 fax: 520 49 28
satis@kaknus.com.tr
www.kaknus.com.tr /kaknusyayinevi

CONTENTS

THE CHARACTERS

The Prophet Muhammad

He has always been a well-respected man, but can he convince the people of Arabia that he is the Messenger of God?

Abu Talib

Abu Talib loves his nephew Muhammad dearly, but will he stand against the nobles of the Quraysh to protect him?

Khadija

Lady Khadija always knew that her husband Muhammad was special. How can she help him in his task?

The picture next to each character's name shows their name in Arabic calligraphy. The Arabic language has always been very important to Muslims because it is the language of the Qur'an, the holy book of Islam, and decorative writing has always been a valued form of art in Muslim culture.

Ali

Ali was brought up by his older cousin, Muhammad, and has always admired him. But can Ali risk his own life for Muhammad?

Abu Bakr

Abu Bakr believed in the message of his friend Muhammad immediately. How can he encourage others to believe in it too?

Aisha

The Prophet Muhammad's second wife Lady Aisha, Abu Bakr's daughter, has an excellent memory. How will she help the Muslims?

Nobles of the Quraysh

The Quraysh are the ruling class of Mecca, and receive lots of money from pilgrims coming to worship. Why do they reject the message that the Prophet Muhammad brings?

Bahira watched the travellers making their way through the desert (*see page 11*).

THE PROPHET MUHAMMAD

(upon him be peace and blessings)

A gentle breeze blew over the town of Mecca, at the heart of the Arabian Peninsula, as Abd al-Muttalib approached the sacred shrine of the Kaaba. Old Abd al-Muttalib was pensive, thinking about his son, his beloved Abdullah, who had died seven months earlier, only two months after marrying Amina. Yet Abdullah had left behind a memory with Amina, and this was the night she would deliver her baby.

Abd al-Muttalib reached the Kaaba, where he asked God to grant him a fine grandson to make up for the loss of his son. As dawn broke, he heard hurrying footsteps. He looked up to see Amina's maid rushing towards him.

'My lady has given birth to a boy!' she exclaimed joyfully.

When he reached Amina's house, Abd al-Muttalib congratulated Amina on the delivery of her baby, and leaned to kiss his little, radiant forehead.

‘What name should he be given?’ asked Amina.

Abd al-Muttalib gave no answer, but rose with the baby in his arms. Blissfully cradling his grandson, he went immediately to the Kaaba and walked around it, thanking God for this tremendous gift. Many possible names came to his mind, but eventually the child’s name was inspired to him in his heart: Muhammad. This would be the baby’s name. The name had never been used by the Arabs before, but now Muhammad, the pride of the universe, had entered the world.

صلى الله عليه وسلم

Wet nurses from the desert came to Mecca seeking babies to look after. It was normal for

wealthy city families to give their babies to women from the desert to nurse them and bring them up. Both families gained from this custom - the desert family received gifts and good treatment from the baby's father, and the child was brought up in the clean desert environment, away from pollution and diseases. What's more, everybody admired the Bedouin from the desert for their strong, independent character and their mastery of the beautiful classical Arabic language. The city families wanted their children to absorb this traditional culture.

One of the wet nurses was Halima, a poor woman from the tribe of Bani Saad. The Quraysh, the wealthy ruling tribe in Mecca, didn't want to give any of their babies to Halima because they were worried about entrusting their children to such a poor woman, and none of the other wet nurses wanted to take Muhammad because they knew that, as his father had died, they would not receive anything in return. Having no other choice, Halima took this auspicious baby.

Halima would later recount with amazement how her life had entirely changed when she began to look after the boy. 'As soon as I stepped out into the desert with Muhammad,' she would say, 'we were showered with God's bounty. Whenever our sheep went out to the pastures, they would return full of milk, even though the sheep of my fellow Bedouin came back hungry and with very little milk.'

After spending several years with Halima, it was finally time for Muhammad to return to his mother. Halima didn't want him to go, and held him tightly as she said goodbye.

صلى الله عليه وسلم

When Muhammad was six years old, his mother Amina took him to Yathrib, an oasis two hundred and fifty miles north of Mecca, to visit relatives. On the way back to Mecca, Amina fell ill and died in a village called al-Abwa.

So Abd al-Muttalib took it upon himself to raise his beloved grandson, showering him with love and affection. However, Beloved Muhammad's happiness was not to last. Two years after the death of his mother, his grandfather also passed away. He was left in the care of his uncle Abu Talib, who was a well-respected member of the Quraysh. The Noble Muhammad moved to Abu Talib's house and as long as he lived there, his uncle and his aunt, Fatima, were always very kind to him and treated him as one of their own children.

When Muhammad was twelve, Abu Talib agreed to take him on a business journey to Syria. On their way, they passed the cell of a Christian monk called Bahira. It was unusual for Bahira to watch caravans and travelers, but when he saw this blessed group making their way through the desert, he decided to invite them for a stopover. When he met Muhammad, he realized that here was the prophet who had been described in the Christian books. He uncovered Muhammad's back and saw, as he was expecting, a mark as big as an apple, which was the seal of prophethood.

'Tremendous things are in store for this boy!' he cried with excitement.

He told Abu Talib to abandon the trip, and return with Muhammad to Mecca, where he should take very good care of him.

صلى الله عليه وسلم

By the time Muhammad was twenty-five, everybody called him 'al-Amin', which means 'the trustworthy'. He had been working as a trader for several years, and it was clear that he was very different from everyone around him. He was always honest and fair in his dealings, and never engaged in merchants' tricks, which were all too common at the time. Muhammad was invariably thoughtful and full of compassion. He was a paragon of elegance and nobility.

One of the merchants in Mecca was a wealthy woman called Khadija. She had outlived two

husbands, and being an experienced trader herself, she now employed men to trade on her behalf. She had heard good things about 'al-Amin', so chose him as a reliable person to sell some goods for her in Syria. Khadija sent her servant Maysara to Syria with Muhammad, and when they returned, Maysara reported that al-Amin really was a most excellent person.

Khadija was an intelligent, determined and noble woman. She thought very hard about Muhammad, this unusually truthful and decisive man with his thick wavy hair and beard, and remembered the way his face always had a special glow. She decided to ask him to marry her.

Muhammad was surprised when he heard Khadija's proposal, but he was very pleased. They were married and in due course had six children – Qasim, Zaynab, Ruqayya, Umm Kulthum, Fatima and Abdullah. They were a happy family, though there were also times of sadness, as both Qasim and Abdullah died in infancy.

صلى الله عليه وسلم

At that time, most of the people of Arabia believed in many gods. There was the High God, al-Lah, and there were also many lesser gods, including al-Lat, al-Uzza and Manat. Idols had been put inside and around the Kaaba, the shrine that had originally been built by the Prophet Abraham with the help of his son the Prophet Isma'il for the worship of the one true God. People came from far and wide to pray and make offerings to the idols there.

Muhammad was convinced that these practices were wrong.

'How can a person worship a lifeless stone that can't help or harm anyone?' he wondered.

صلى الله عليه وسلم

When Muhammad was thirty-five years old, a great flood swept through Mecca. It destroyed many of the houses and damaged the Kaaba. The Quraysh decided that each clan should be given a section of the Kaaba to rebuild, so that they could all take part in the noble task. When they got to the stage of placing the sacred Black Stone, a fierce argument broke out about who would have the honor of putting it in its final position.

As the quarrelling voices got louder and louder, a Quraysh noble called out a suggestion. 'Let's ask the first man who comes through the gate what to do.'

They all agreed. Soon after, a figure appeared at the gate.

'Oh! It's Muhammad the trustworthy! We'll accept his judgement!' they exclaimed.

Muhammad listened carefully to the cause of their argument and asked for a cloak. He laid it on the ground and put the Black Stone in the middle of it.

‘Each clan must hold onto an edge of the cloak,’ he explained calmly, ‘and all shall carry it together.’

In this way, everybody carried the Black Stone, and Muhammad placed it in its final position himself.

صلى الله عليه وسلم

Muhammad began to leave the busy city of Mecca regularly to go into the mountains; he wanted to get away from the bustle and noise of town life and be closer to God. He would take a little food and water with him.

He thought deeply about how much he disliked the way that the Quraysh worshipped so many gods and idols. It was very different from how he felt people’s relationship with God should be. The way the people around him lived their lives also deeply worried him. There were far too many violent struggles between the different tribes, and everybody seemed to be desperate to gain money and power, even if that meant hurting the weakest people, including widows and orphans.

When he was forty years old, in the month of Ramadan, the ninth month of the lunar year, he climbed high up into the Mountain of Light (Nur) above Mecca and entered the cave of Hira, his favorite hideaway. One night he was again lost in contemplation. Suddenly the angel Gabriel appeared and commanded, 'Recite!' (*Iqra'*!)

Muhammad was stunned at the sight of the angel. 'I'm not of those who can recite,' he answered in awe.

The angel Gabriel held him so tightly that he felt he couldn't bear it any longer. Then the angel released him and repeated the divine command, 'Recite!'

Trying to remain composed, Muhammad repeated, 'I cannot recite.'

The angel held him tightly once again until Muhammad felt that almost all breath in him had been squeezed out. Then the angel released him a second time, giving him the first ever revelation: 'Recite in the name of your Lord, who created man from a clot of congealed blood. Recite, for your Lord is most generous and taught by the pen, teaching man that which he knew not.'

By this time the Prophet Muhammad was shivering and in a state of profound shock. It was all that he could do to stand up and stagger away from the mouth of the cave. When Khadija saw him, she could tell something utterly bewildering had happened to him. It was as if he had a fever.

'What's the matter?' she asked, reaching out to him. 'Where have you been?'

'Cover me! Cover me!' he begged her.

Khadija wrapped him in a thick cloak and held him closely, wondering what had happened.

When the Prophet Muhammad became calmer, he told her what he had seen and heard, and how afraid he had been. 'Don't be scared,' said Khadija confidently. 'You are a good man. God will never let you down.'

Khadija suggested that they ask the opinion of her cousin Waraqa, a wise Christian who knew a lot about holy scriptures. When Waraqa heard the story, his face burst into a delighted smile. He confirmed to Khadija what she had already suspected: Muhammad had seen the angel of revelation - therefore he must be a prophet!

Lady Khadija was the first person to believe that the Prophet Muhammad brought a divine invitation from God, and was thus the first Muslim. She gave her husband, the Prophet, strength and support, and helped him in every way she could for the rest of her life.

After that day, the Prophet Muhammad received a great number of revelations from the Angel Gabriel. The Holy Prophet had been granted a great power to be able to bear, recite and teach the divine revelation; the kind of power no other human being had ever been or would ever be given. The verses he recited were gathered together and became the Quran.

صلى الله عليه وسلم

God revealed to the Prophet Muhammad that there was only one God, the God that Abraham had worshipped. The Prophet was taught through the revealed verses of the Quran that all human beings should surrender themselves to God, which meant that every single thing in their lives, including money and fame, should take second place to Him. The Prophet was told that everyone is equal before God - men, women, rich people, poor people and slaves, and it makes no difference which family you come from. When people die, they are judged for what they have done during their lives, so it is very important that they should be good and treat everybody else well, particularly those who are weaker and poorer than themselves.

It was also revealed to the Prophet Muhammad that Muslims should stay close to God through regular prayers. Gabriel showed the Prophet exactly how Muslims should pray, and how they should ritually wash themselves in a particular way before performing their five daily prayers.

The Prophet shared the teachings with his closest companions. To begin with, Khadija, the mother of the believers, prayed with him, and they were soon joined by their daughters, Zaynab, Ruqayya, Umm Kulthum and Fatima. Ali, Abu Talib's son, who was being raised in the Prophet's household, also joined them, as did Zayd, a young man who had been the Prophet's slave. Umm Ayman, one of the Prophet's nursemaids from when he was a child, came to pray, as did Abu Bakr, his closest friend. Thus the Holy Prophet began to share his message from God with those he could trust.

Abu Bakr was a popular merchant in Mecca, and people often came to talk to him. 'Have you heard that Muhammad is the Prophet of God?' he asked them enthusiastically. 'The angel Gabriel came to Muhammad to tell him that God has power over everything in our lives, and we mustn't ever forget that. When we die, our money and the things that we own can't help us. We must look after everybody who needs help. Then God will make us happy after we die.'

The new Muslims met regularly in secret to pray and learn from the Prophet about the new religion. They were men and women from all the different clans. Some of them were rich, but many of them were poor and treated badly by those around them. They liked the idea that everybody was equal before God, and that the weaker people in society should be helped.

Three years after the first revelation, the Prophet Muhammad received a revelation from God telling him to now share the new religion with everyone. He climbed up to the top of Mount Safa and urgently shouted out the names of all the nobles. Thinking there was a crisis in the city, everybody quickly gathered at the bottom of the mountain.

'If I were to warn you that there were horsemen in this other valley about to attack you, would you believe me?' he called down to them.

'Yes,' they replied together. 'We have never heard you lie.'

'I have been ordered to warn you that terrible things will happen to you if you do not believe in the one God!' he cried out, his voice filling the valley.

There was a second of silence. Then Abu Lahab, one of the oldest in the crowd as well as an uncle of the Prophet, shouted out angrily, 'Woe to you! Did you really gather us here to tell us this nonsense?'

Abu Lahab elbowed his way through the crowd, his face red. The people in the crowd were confused and worried. Who were they supposed to believe? Gradually they walked away. The Prophet was left alone. How would he ever convince people of his message from God?

صلى الله عليه وسلم

The Prophet and the Muslims now began to call to and teach Islam openly. They told the people that the gods and idols of the old religion weren't real. This made the leaders of the Quraysh angrier and angrier. The idols in the Kaaba brought many pilgrims to Mecca, and the money these pilgrims spent there made the nobles rich. If the Prophet convinced everybody that the idols were worthless, the Quraysh would lose money, power and status.

The leaders of the Quraysh visited Abu Talib several times to order him to force his nephew to stop preaching. Abu Talib tried to reach a compromise with his beloved nephew, but when he realized that the Prophet would never stop trying to share the new religion, he gave up. Instead he promised that he would always protect him, even though he didn't become a Muslim himself.

Some Muslims who didn't belong to powerful clans and families were beaten and tortured by people who wanted to convince them to stop following the new religion, and to scare other people from joining it. The first person to be tortured to death because she was a Muslim was a lady called

Sumayya. She was the mother of the famous companion of the Prophet, the Noble Ammar.

The Prophet hated to see the Muslims suffering. He secretly organized for two groups of them to go by boat to Abyssinia, where there was a Christian king who was well known for being kind and just. When the leaders of the Quraysh found out that some of the Muslims had secretly left Mecca, they were furious. They quickly sent men with gifts to Abyssinia to convince the king to send the Muslims back, but the king, on hearing a verse from the Quran about Jesus and his mother Mary, wiped tears from his eyes and told the Muslims that they didn't have to go back to Mecca. They could stay in Abyssinia and live in peace.

The Quraysh regularly tried to upset the Prophet and make his life miserable, often by doing all sorts of dastardly, ignoble things like putting thorns on the path where he was about to walk. One day, Abu Jahl, a leader of the Quraysh, shouted out insults about Islam as he walked past the Prophet. The Prophet ignored him and looked the other way. Hamza, the Prophet's uncle, was the strongest man in the Quraysh at the time. He wasn't a Muslim yet, but he did love and respect his nephew dearly. That day he was returning from yet another hunting trip in the desert and was striding along the street near the Kaaba with his bow and arrow when a woman called out to tell him about these insults. Hamza immediately felt himself boiling with anger. He set off at a run to find Abu Jahl, and when he found him he hit him hard with his bow. 'How dare you insult Muhammad when I'm also upon his religion!' Hamza's hatred of disrespect and his desire to support his nephew led him to convert to Islam there and then.

Hearing the commotion, people gathered around to help Abu Jahl. Holding his head, he brushed them off, muttering, ‘Leave Hamza alone; I admit that I did insult his nephew badly.’

The addition of the powerful Hamza to the Muslims made them stronger. The Quraysh knew that Hamza would try to protect the Prophet, so they stopped insulting him so much.

Umar ibn al-Khattab was another man in Mecca at the time who was widely feared and respected for his tremendous courage. He decided to kill the Prophet, but when he heard verses of the Qur’an he was so struck by them that he immediately embraced the new faith.

Now that Hamza and Umar were on their side, the Muslims were now able to pray openly at the Kaaba.

صلى الله عليه وسلم

When they found that they couldn’t convince the Prophet to give up his teaching by insulting him and threatening him, the Quraysh became very frustrated. The Muslims wouldn’t abandon their new religion even when they were beaten. They didn’t even fight back. They continued to pray, and to say

that they believed that there was only one God and that Muhammad was God's Messenger.

'The only solution is to make the Muslims so hungry and isolated that they will beg to return to the old ways,' the Quraysh agreed.

So a notice was put up at the Kaaba saying that everybody had to avoid the Muslims and the Prophet's clan, and that nobody could trade with them. The Muslims became hungrier and hungrier, and poorer and poorer.

Eventually, after two long years, some of the Muslims' relations managed to put an end to the boycott. When they went to the Kaaba to tear down the notice they found that all the words on it had been eaten by worms, except for 'In Your Name, O God'.

صلى الله عليه وسلم

The Prophet's joy at being able to live and trade as before suddenly came to an end. Khadija, his dear wife and greatest supporter, died. She had always encouraged him and supported his mission in any way she could.

Several months after Khadija died, Abu Talib also passed away. The Prophet felt desperately sad at the loss of his kind uncle, who had always tried to protect him, even though they didn't share the same religion.

The Prophet and the Muslims were now in more danger than ever before. They didn't have Abu Talib preventing the Quraysh from harming them. People threw dirt in the Prophet's face and he wondered how long it would be before they did worse.

صلى الله عليه وسلم

The Prophet realized that it was time to share the message from God with people outside Mecca. He went to the green and beautiful town of Taif and spoke there about Islam, but nobody wanted to listen. People shouted insults and had their children throw stones at him.

The Prophet felt overwhelmed with grief. He found a quiet place in a shady orchard and prayed urgently to God. All the terrible things that were happening to them caused him immense grief, but he trusted entirely that God was in control of his life and would choose what was best for him in the end.

صلى الله عليه وسلم

Soon after, the Prophet was given some relief from his sadness by a new experience. He had returned to Mecca. Some days later, when he was resting one night in his cousin Umm Khani's house, which was near the Kaaba, suddenly the Angel Gabriel came and woke him up, and showed him a most magnificent white winged beast.

'This is Buraq,' the angel Gabriel told the Prophet.

The Prophet climbed on Buraq, and with the angel next to him he found himself taken out of Mecca, high across the Arabian Peninsula, and north to the holy city of Jerusalem. The long journey that would normally have taken weeks took just a few moments.

They arrived at Jerusalem's great al-Aqsa Mosque. There, the Prophet Muhammad met the prophets who had come before him - Abraham, Moses and Jesus and more - and led them in prayer, which symbolizes the fact that he is the last in the long line of prophets.

Then the Prophet Muhammad mounted Buraq again, and Gabriel led them from the mosque up through the clouds, higher and higher, until they had passed through all the heavens. The Prophet finally met God, who spoke to him. Among the things God directly revealed to him that night were the five prescribed daily prayers that each and every Muslim who has reached puberty must observe without fail.

Buraq then carried Muhammad back to Mecca. Amazingly it was still night-time when they arrived and furthermore his bed was still warm.

The Night Journey to Jerusalem (*Isra*) and the Ascension to the Heavens (*Mi'rāj*) gave the Prophet Muhammad great comfort and a feeling of calmness. It gave him new energy after the long months of loneliness and struggle he had endured.

صلى الله عليه وسلم

Every year pilgrims from all over the Arabian Peninsula took part in a pilgrimage to the Kaaba in Mecca. Some pilgrims from the city of Yathrib had heard about the Prophet and his new religion, and when they came to Mecca on their pilgrimage they asked him about it. They were quickly convinced that he really was the Messenger of God, and became Muslims immediately. They explained that the fighting between the tribes around Yathrib was destroying them. Perhaps, they suggested, God had sent the Prophet Muhammad to bring the tribes together again.

Two years later, more pilgrims from Yathrib came to speak to the Prophet. They met in secret at night on a hill called Aqaba. In the moonlight the leaders from Yathrib told the Prophet that if he and the Meccan Muslims came to Yathrib, the people of Yathrib would be loyal to and protect him as well as the Muslims.

The Prophet replied, 'I am yours and you are mine. I will fight anybody that you fight. I will make peace with anybody you make peace with.'

At last the Prophet and the Muslims were no longer alone.

صلى الله عليه وسلم

During the summer of that year the Muslims began quietly to leave Mecca to go to live in Yathrib. Before long all the Prophet's closest companions had gone except for Abu Bakr and Ali, who stayed with him in Mecca.

The Quraysh had been becoming more and more worried that the Prophet was gaining power and followers, and they called a meeting to discuss how to stop him. They decided that he had to be killed. Abu Jahl came up with the plan that a young, powerful noble from each clan should strike the Prophet at exactly the same moment. At that time the law decreed that when one person murdered another, the clan of the victim would seek revenge on the tribe of the murderer. But if all the men killed Muhammad at precisely the same second, his clan wouldn't be able to attack all the other clans. In this way they would be able to get rid of their "chief enemy" without putting themselves in danger.

It was settled. After night had fallen, the young nobles gathered outside the blessed house of the Prophet and waited for him to leave for the Morning Prayer. One of them peered through the shutters and saw a sleeping figure covered in the Prophet's green cloak.

He returned to the others and whispered confidently, 'Muhammad is inside, and he's fast asleep. He'll be out soon.'

But when the morning came, still nobody had left the house. Suddenly the door swung open. The nobles gripped their weapons, their hearts pounding. But rather than the Prophet that they were expecting to find, out strode Ali, all alone. The Prophet had left during the night without any of them seeing.

He had gone immediately to Abu Bakr's house, and the two of them had set off together into the mountains. They knew that as soon as the Quraysh realized that the Prophet had left Mecca, they would do their best to find him and kill him. They went to a cave in the mountain of Thawr to the south of Mecca, as part of their strategy.

Abu Bakr's son, Abdullah, came to them with news of what was being said about them in Mecca, and his daughter Asma brought them food.

Three days later the Prophet and his truthful and loyal confidant Abu Bakr heard some of the Quraysh searching for them near the cave. The Quraysh had been led there by their guide, who had seen that the tracks he was following had stopped at the mouth of the cave. So they all went to check out the cave. When they drew near, they noticed that a spider had made its web over the mouth of the cave and two doves were nesting in front of it.

'They're very close,' whispered Abu Bakr fearing for the life of the Prophet. 'If one of them looks down, he'll see us.'

The Prophet remained perfectly calm. 'Don't have any grief,' he assured his friend. 'What do

you think of two people whose third is God? God is with us.'

On seeing the spider web and the nest of the doves, the Quraysh agreed that it was impossible for anybody to be inside this particular cave, and moved on.

Once they were sure that the coastal route was clear, the Prophet and Abu Bakr found their camels again and resumed their journey to Yathrib.

They were sure that the Quraysh would be keeping close watch on the direct route from Mecca to Yathrib, so, using a guide, Abdullah ibn

Urayqit, who was not yet a Muslim but was well known for being trustworthy, they set off south-west, away from Yathrib. When they felt safe enough, they turned northwards along the coast, back towards their destination. The Quraysh never imagined that they would choose such an unusual route, so they could not find them.

The Prophet Muhammad's journey from Mecca to Yathrib became known as the Hijra, or the Emigration, and the year in which it took place, 622 of the Christian calendar, became Year 1 of the Muslim calendar.

صلى الله عليه وسلم

The Prophet Muhammad was greeted in Yathrib with great festivities, songs and cries of 'God is greatest!' Everybody wanted him to stay with them. He didn't want it to seem that he preferred one family over another, so he let go of the reins of his camel and said that he would live wherever the camel chose.

Everybody watched with excitement as the camel wandered through the streets. Eventually it settled at a piece of land where there was a barn used for drying dates. This was where the Prophet chose to build his home and a mosque. Both were built very simply, as the Prophet explained that money should not be spent on luxury items, but on helping the poor and needy. The mosque was used for prayer and also for public meetings. People of all religions and from all tribes would come and talk to the Prophet about their problems, and he would give them advice.

The city of Yathrib became known as Medina, a short form of Medinat al-Nabi, or 'the city of the Prophet'. When the Muslims and the Prophet came to Medina, the new community of believers was called the 'umma'. The relationships in Medina between people of different religions and tribes needed to be clear, so the Prophet made a treaty that set out everybody's rights and duties. Muslims would be judged according to the laws of Islam, and non-Muslims would be judged using their own laws and would be free to continue with their own religions. However, if the Muslims or their allies were attacked, everybody had a duty to join together to protect each other.

The Muslims prayed five times a day, and as the times of these prayers depended on the position of the sun in the sky, which changed throughout the year, they needed to be told just before each prayer time. Abdullah ibn Zayd came to the Prophet and reported that he had been taught the words of the 'azan', the call to prayer, in a dream. Umar ibn al-Khattab, who was also present, said that he had been shown the exact same dream. The Prophet confirmed the validity of their dreams and gave the honor of being the first person to call Muslims to prayer to Bilal, a black Abyssinian slave who had suffered greatly in Mecca for being a Muslim, who had later been bought and freed by Abu Bakr.

After Khadija's death, the Prophet married several wives, as was normal at the time. His favorite wife was Abu Bakr's daughter, Aisha. She was intelligent and lively, and she wasn't afraid to ask questions or tell others her opinions. She watched carefully how the Prophet behaved and she remembered everything he told her about Islam and his life. The Prophet trusted the knowledge of Aisha so much that he told the believers that they should take half (or a third of) their religious knowledge from her.

Aisha would continue to share her memories of the Prophet's words and actions with others long after the Prophet had passed away, and the Muslims used this information to help them decide how God wanted them to behave in all sorts of different circumstances.

Most of the Prophet's other wives were widows of Muslims who had died fighting for Islam, and women from other tribes. By marrying them, he created strong links between the Muslims and the other tribes. His wives lived in small separate cells attached to the mosque so they were at the center of the community, and would often discuss current affairs and religious and political issues with him.

Verses of the Qur'an revealed that women had the same religious rights and responsibilities as men, and that they should receive their own inheritance, which had not happened before.

صلى الله عليه وسلم

Although the Muslims were now protected in Medina, it was clear that they needed to gain power again in Mecca if Islam was to become a strong religion for everybody, not just for those in the city of Medina.

They thought about how best to weaken the Quraysh's hold over Mecca, and decided that one way would be to raid the Quraysh's trade caravans travelling between Mecca and Syria.

Abu Sufyan, the head of the Quraysh, was heading a large caravan from Syria to Mecca when he was told that the Muslims were planning to ambush it. He sent a message to the Quraysh in Mecca asking for help. The caravan made it safely to Mecca, but the Quraysh had sent an army of a thousand men to attack the Muslims. The Muslims gathered a force of just over three hundred men and a battle broke out near the wells of Badr. After fierce fighting, the Muslims defeated the Quraysh, not losing many of their own men, but killing a great many members of the Quraysh, including Abu Jahl and several others of the most important leaders.

The Prophet distributed the spoils from the battle fairly between the Muslims, and ordered that all prisoners be treated well. The poor ones could convert to Islam or be sent back to Mecca; the rich ones could convert to Islam or, if a ransom was paid, could return to Mecca. And anybody who taught 10 Muslims to read would also be released. All the new converts to Islam received a share of the booty.

The Muslims returned to Medina joyfully celebrating their incredible victory over the Quraysh army, which had been so much the larger and better equipped. The Quraysh returned to Mecca deeply embarrassed by such a shameful defeat. What should they do now? Should they simply accept the death of so many of their notable members?

صلى الله عليه وسلم

Early the next year the Muslims found out that the Quraysh were preparing to fight them again. The two sides met at Uhud. The Muslims positioned themselves just in front of the mountain so they could not be attacked from behind. The Prophet put archers on the top of the hill and told

them to defend the Muslims and not to leave their positions no matter what happened. Again there were many more warriors from the Quraysh than there were Muslims, but the Muslims fought hard and looked like they were about to win.

Most of the archers left their positions, thinking that the victory had been won, although they had been strictly instructed by the Prophet. The Quraysh horsemen, led by the heroic young commander of the Quraysh, Khalid ibn al-Walid, who had not yet become a Muslim, seized this moment to charge at the Muslims from behind. Great confusion ensued and many Muslims were martyred, including Hamza, the Prophet's beloved, leonine uncle. And in this moment of great confusion, one of the enemy killed a companion who he thought was the Prophet.

"Muhammad has been killed!" he shouted and some of the companions who heard his cry lost heart and scattered away.

Just a few companions stayed to defend the Prophet, who had been injured. Among these was Nusayba, a woman who had been bringing water to the Muslim fighters.

When she saw the Prophet, she seized a sword and began to defend him fiercely. The Prophet saw that she had no shield, so shouted to one of the fleeing men, 'Give your shield to the one who is fighting!'

The man threw it to Nusayba and she continued with her sword, striking the enemy through their double armor and causing a horse and its rider to fall. In turn she was attacked by horsemen and received thirteen wounds, including one in her neck that took a year to heal.

The Quraysh dealt the believers a heavy blow indeed but were still unable to attain their goal of putting out the sun of Islam. The Muslims returned to Medina bitterly disappointed and with great sadness at the loss of family and friends.

Two years after Uhud, the Quraysh and their allies marched towards the Muslims again, this time with a far greater army. A famous companion of Persian origin, Salman al-Farisi, suggested digging a trench to better protect themselves. The Prophet liked his idea, hence the name, the Battle of the Trench (Khandak). The Muslims dug a trench along the least protected edge of the city to stop the enemy getting in. Everybody took part in the digging, including the Prophet himself.

When the Muslims' enemies saw the long and wide trench, they were confused. How could they cross it? The Quraysh and those with them tried to cross the trench, but they couldn't find a way.

It was at this point that the Qurayzah, an ally of the Muslims and the only Jewish tribe left in Medina since the two other Jewish tribes had themselves expelled due a number of treacherous acts, decided to change their loyalty and connive with the enemies of the Muslims outside the city. The Muslims, who could not leave their city for fear of attack, had almost run out of food and now had enemies both outside and within.

The Prophet prayed to God for something to change so that the Muslims would not all be killed and the message of Islam lost.

Suddenly an enormous sandstorm blew up, which lasted for days. The Quraysh and their allies didn't know what to do. Their animals were dying, their equipment and belongings were being ruined, and they couldn't prepare any food to eat. It was impossible to fight in these conditions, so they set off, back to Mecca.

Although the siege of Medina had been lifted, the Muslims still had to deal with the Qurayzah, who had broken the agreement of loyalty they had made with the Muslims. The Prophet allowed the Qurayzah to choose who would judge them, and they chose a man from the tribe of Aws who had always had a good relationship with the Qurayzah: Sa'd ibn Muadh, who had been fatally wounded during the siege. He declared that, according to the Qurayzah's own laws, which was the Jewish law, they had to be punished. All their men should be killed, all the women and children taken as prisoners, and all their belongings divided between the Muslims.

صلى الله عليه وسلم

The Muslims in Medina longed to make a pilgrimage to Mecca and visit the Kaaba, so the Prophet decided that they should make an attempt. He set off with 1,400 Muslims on a pilgrimage to Mecca. When the Quraysh found out about it, they feared that the Muslims would try to take control of the city if they were allowed in.

The Muslims left Medina armed only with travelers' daggers, and travelled south towards Mecca. At the wells of Hudaybiyya they stopped and waited. Some of the Quraysh came out to meet them to discuss what should happen, and eventually the Treaty of Hudaybiyya was made. It was agreed that the Muslims would not be allowed to continue their pilgrimage to Mecca that year, but they could return the following year and safely visit the Kaaba. The treaty said that there should be no war between the two sides for ten years, and that people should be free to choose to join forces either with the Prophet and the Muslims, or with the Quraysh.

The Muslims had written into the treaty the words 'Muhammad, Prophet of God', but the Quraysh insisted that 'Muhammad, son of Abdullah' be put instead. The Muslims were outraged at this lack of respect, but the Prophet Muhammad calmed them. He pointed out that words didn't need to be written in a treaty for them to remain true.

Many Muslims were angry and disappointed at the terms of the treaty, but the Prophet reminded them that the Qur'an taught that if the Muslims' enemies offered peace, the Muslims always had to agree. Peace was always better than war.

Later that day, God revealed a new verse of the Qur'an that confirmed that the treaty had indeed been a great victory for the Muslims. They had shown that not only did they have sincere faith, but also that they were humble and calm, showed mercy, and could control themselves.

According to the Treaty of Hudaybiyya, there could be no fighting for ten years. However, soon after the treaty was signed the tribe of Bakr, an ally of the Quraysh, attacked the tribe of Khuza'a, an ally of the Muslims. The Quraysh supported the tribe of Bakr, and in doing so breached the Treaty of Hudaybiyya.

صلى الله عليه وسلم

The Prophet now set out to Mecca with the largest force of Muslims that had ever been gathered. The Quraysh were afraid. They had spent thirteen years insulting and hurting the Muslims when they were living in Mecca, and they had spent eight years fighting the Muslims after they had moved to Medina. Now they had broken an important peace treaty, how would the Muslims treat them? Would they seek revenge?

The army of Muslims entered Mecca and took control of the city quite peacefully. The Prophet Muhammad put up his red tent near the Kaaba. He entered the sacred precinct on his camel with his forehead almost touching the back of the camel and in that great humility performed the circumambulation. He thanked God for the Muslims' victory. He then gathered the people of Mecca together.

‘O Quraysh,’ he cried. ‘What do you think I should do with you?’

‘We hope for the best,’ they replied. ‘You are a noble brother.’

‘Go your own ways!’ said Muhammad. ‘There is no blaming you today, you are all free.’ The Prophet had decided that the Quraysh should be forgiven for what they had done to the Muslims in the past. Many decided to become Muslims, but they were not forced to do so.

The Muslims rejoiced that they were finally able to worship at the Kaaba again. The Prophet entered the Kaaba together with Ali, his beloved son-in-law, and together they destroyed all the idols defiling the holy house of God. The shrine became dedicated once and for all to the worship of the one true God.

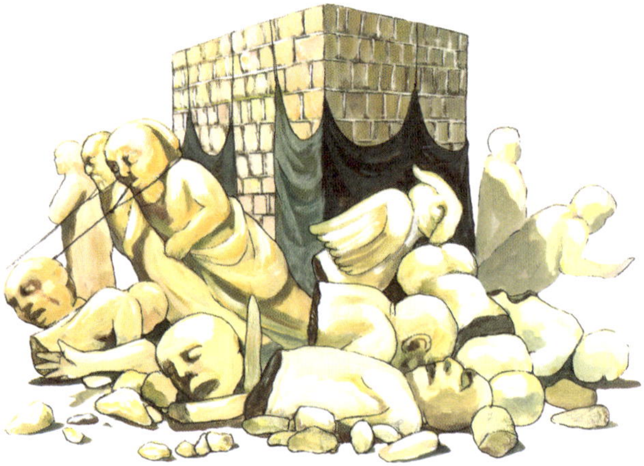

The arrival of the Muslims in Mecca did not please everybody in Arabia. The Muslims continued to fight battles to make sure that there were no immediate threats against Islam. More and more people decided to become Muslims, and more and more tribes travelled to Medina to swear that they would be loyal to Muhammad.

صلى الله عليه وسلم

Ten years after the Hijra, the Prophet Muhammad decided to lead the hajj – his one and only - the official pilgrimage to Mecca that is still an essential duty of every able Muslim. The Prophet demonstrated to the Muslims what they should do on their pilgrimage, and explained to them the meaning of each action.

He gathered all the Muslims together near Mount Arafat. The crowd was vast, and everybody jostled with each other to get a glimpse of the Prophet. By now he was almost 62 years old and knew that this would probably be his last chance to address so many Muslims in this way. When the crowd was quiet, the Prophet began to speak.

He reminded them of everything that Islam had taught them, that they should praise God, be kind and fair to everyone, and not fight each other. 'Have I faithfully delivered my message to you?' he asked at the end.

'Yes, you have!' the crowd roared, and the echo of their voices rolled around the valley.

صلى الله عليه وسلم

Two months after the pilgrimage, the Prophet fell ill. He breathed his last in Aisha's arms and was buried near her house. He had devoted the last twenty-three years to inviting people to the truth and encouraging them to believe in one God, to put their total trust in Him, and to make Him their priority over everything else. The Prophet had taught people that they would be rewarded or punished for their actions in this life. Everybody is equal before God, and it makes no difference whether they are men or women, what color they are, which family they belong to, or how rich or poor they are. The only way one person can be better than another is by loving God more, and by showing this love in the way they live their life.

TAKING THINGS FURTHER

The real read

This Real Reads volume of *Muhammad: The Life of the Prophet* is our interpretation of the events in the life of the Prophet Muhammad.

In writing this account, we have relied closely on many original sources, mainly Ibn Ishaq's biography of the Prophet. As Ibn Ishaq died in 767, his biography is thought to be one of the earliest and most reliable accounts of the Prophet's life. Ibn Ishaq's actual text has been lost, but we know most of what he wrote from reading the work of Ibn Hisham, who produced an edited version of Ibn Ishaq's biography of which copies still exist today.

Even the earliest biographies of the Prophet we have were written over a hundred years after he died, and the differences between them can be puzzling. Sometimes the details of his life vary considerably between different biographies, and there are sometimes even different versions of the same event in the same biography.

As centuries went by, Muslim scholars wanted to write down and clarify what the Prophet

Muhammad had said and done in as many aspects of daily life as possible, both as a record of the key events in Muslim history and as guidance in how to live as close to God as possible.

These scholars collected the *hadiths*, the sayings of the Prophet, and memories of his *sunna*, his behavior, that had been passed down through the generations. It was clear that some of these *hadiths* could be trusted more than others, so each saying came with a list of the people who had passed it on. A detailed science developed to study these people and their lives. Sometimes the scholars found, for example, that it was impossible for a certain person to have heard a *hadith*, so they judged that Muslims couldn't trust that *hadith*. One of the most famous scholars of *hadiths* was al-Bukhari. Lady Aisha, mother of the believers, narrated thousands of hadiths along with a number of key companions in the science of hadith narration, such as Abu Hurayrah, Jabir ibn Abdillah, Abdullah ibn Abbas, and Abdullah ibn Mas'ud.

Scholars used the *hadiths* and the *sunna*, along with the Quran, to develop the *sharia* - Islamic law.

The Prophet Muhammad

It is recommended that Muslims always offer a short prayer for the Prophet Muhammad after saying his name, usually 'May God's peace and blessings be upon him'. In Arabic the prayer looks like this and is pronounced *salla Allahu alayhi wa sallam.* Between the sections of the text in this book we have an Arabic calligraphic device which elaborates on this prayer by adding beautiful decorations.

Pictures of the Prophet Muhammad and the other Islamic prophets, including Abraham, Moses and Jesus, have always been forbidden in Islam. This is because Muslims believe that the prophets were very special people, so only God can know everything about them. If humans were to make an image of a prophet, they would need to have as much knowledge as God, which is both impossible and disrespectful.

Another reason for forbidding images of the prophets is to stop Muslims focusing so much on the images that they lose their concentration on God.

Although images of the Prophet Muhammad have never been allowed by the main Muslim authorities, in the past some Persian, Turkish and Indian Muslims have created pictures of him. When they did so, they used the styles of pictures that were common in their countries before Islam came. In those depictions, however, which are mostly miniatures, the face of the Prophet is almost never shown.

Recently some non-Muslims have drawn so-called pictures and cartoons of the Prophet. They say that they are free to write, draw and say whatever they want to. They believe that if there are limits on what you can think and say and draw, it can be dangerous, and that other people do not have the right to say what you can and can't make pictures of. After all, they say, pictures are only pictures.

When non-Muslims draw images of the Prophet Muhammad, many Muslims are upset and angry because they feel that the artists are laughing at their prophet, and indirectly at Muslims themselves. They believe that non¬Muslims should respect what is important to Muslims even if it isn't important to them.

Life in the time of the Prophet Muhammad

The Prophet Muhammad lived in the Arabian Peninsula, an enormous area of harsh desert. Dotted here and there in the expanses of sand were a few oases, which were the only

places with water. Some people lived permanently in these oases, and some lived in the desert as nomads, travelling from place to place. Each person belonged to a tribe, and the tribes often fought each other violently.

Luxury goods such as spices, ivory and fabrics were carried across the desert by camels to be sold in Syria and Byzantium, to the north-west of Arabia. Mecca was a major city on this trade route, so it was always full of merchants and their camels.

Mecca was also the home of the Kaaba, a shrine that had been there for centuries. Most of the tribes believed in many gods, and they came on pilgrimages to worship the idols in the Kaaba. As well as pagans, there were also small Jewish tribes and Christian communities living in Arabia, mostly in the larger towns..

After the death of the Prophet Muhammad

When the Prophet Muhammad passed away, the Muslims discussed who would be the best person to lead the Muslim community now that their prophet was no longer the leader. Abu Bakr was chosen, as he had been one of the first believers and had been close to the Prophet for most of his life.

After Abu Bakr died, he was succeeded by Umar, and then by Uthman. When Uthman was killed in 656 BCE, Ali became the fourth rightly guided caliph.

After the death of the Prophet Muhammad, the Muslims very quickly gained an enormous empire that stretched from India in the east to Spain in the west. A great many people chose to become Muslims, but those who decided not to, continued to live peacefully in this empire, practicing their own religion, though they had to pay a different kind of tax from the one the Muslims paid.

Finding out more

We recommend the following books, websites and films to gain a greater understanding of the life of the Prophet Muhammad.

Books

- *Muhammad: A Prophet for our Time*, Karen Armstrong, 2006.

- *The Story of Islam*, Rob Lloyd Jones, 2007.
- *Tell Me About the Prophet Mohammad*, Saniyasnain Khan, Goodword Books, 2000.

Websites

- www.plainislam.com
Lots of information about Islam in everyday life.

- www.quran.com
Here you can listen to the Qur'an being recited by different people.

TV and film

- *Inside Mecca*, National Geographic, 2003.
A documentary following several Muslims as they take part in the hajj.

Food for thought

Here are some things to think about if you are reading *Muhammad: The Life of the Prophet* alone, and ideas for discussion if you are reading it with friends.

Starting points

- What qualities did the Prophet Muhammad show when he solved the problem of who would put the Black Stone in position? How do you think he used those qualities later on?

- The Prophet Muhammad chose to go to the mountains to think seriously about life. Where do you find is the best place for you to think about something?

- The Prophet Muhammad and Abu Talib continued to have a close relationship, even though they didn't share the same views. Do you think that it is easy or difficult to be friends with somebody who has different opinions? What are the good things and bad things about a friendship like this?

- Why do you think the Prophet Muhammad forgave the people of Mecca when the Muslims took control of the city? Have you ever forgiven somebody? How did it make you feel?

Group activities

- Town children at the time of the Prophet Muhammad were usually brought up in the desert. Discuss whether you would prefer to be brought up in a house in a town or moving around in the desert. How would this choice affect how you felt about the world?

- Together make a list of all the women in this book. How did they contribute to the life of the Prophet?

- Imagine you are in the crowd during the Prophet's last speech. A foreigner there asks you who the person speaking is. Tell him or her about the Prophet Muhammad's life and what it has meant for you.